ER   Jules, Jacqueline
2-3
JUL   Lights out (Sofia Martinz)

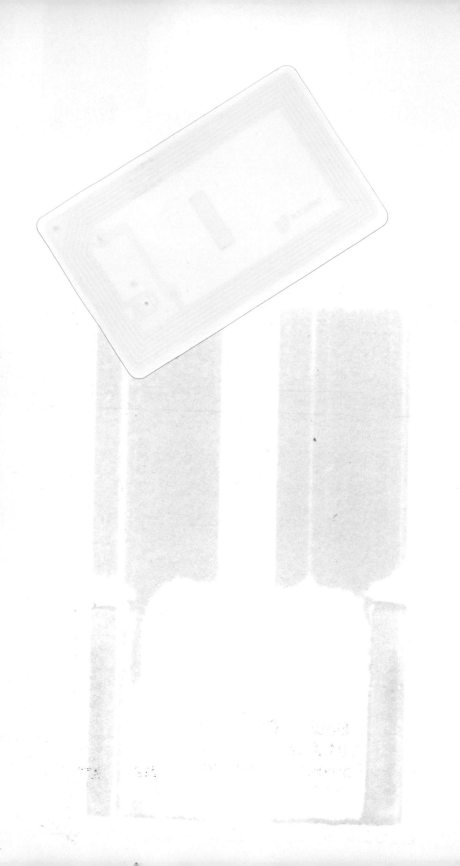

SOFIA MARTINEZ

Lights Out

by Jacqueline Jules

illustrated by Kim Smith

PICTURE WINDOW BOOKS
a capstone imprint

Sofia Martinez is published by
Picture Window Books, a Capstone imprint
1710 Roe Crest Drive
North Mankato, MN 56003
www.mycapstone.com

Library of Congress Cataloging-in-Publication Data
Names: Jules, Jacqueline, 1956- author. | Smith, Kim,
1986- illustrator.

Jules, Jacqueline, 1956- Sofia Martinez.

Title: Lights out / by Jacqueline Jules ; illustrated by
Kim Smith.

Description: North Mankato, Minnesota : Picture
Window Books, a Capstone imprint, 2016 | Series:
Sofia Martinez | Summary: When a storm causes a
neighborhood blackout, Sofia and her father come
up with a plan for the perfect family night without
electricity.

Identifiers: LCCN 2015045738| ISBN 9781479587186
(library binding) | ISBN 9781479587247 (pbk.) | ISBN
9781479587285 (ebook pdf)

Subjects: LCSH: Hispanic American families‹Juvenile
fiction. | Electric power failures‹Juvenile fiction.|
CYAC: Hispanic Americans‹Fiction. |Family
life‹Fiction. | Electric power failures‹Fiction.

Classification: LCC PZ7.J92947 Li 2016 | DDC
813.6‹dc23

LC record available at http://lccn.loc.gov/2015045738

Designer: Kay Fraser

Printed in China.
009465F16

TABLE OF CONTENTS

CHAPTER 1

No Lights

Sofia switched on the light in her bedroom. Nothing happened! She went into the hallway. The light didn't work there, either.

"¡Mamá!" she called.

"Come downstairs," Mamá said.

Sofia found **Mamá**, **Papá**, and her two older sisters, Elena and Luisa, in the kitchen. They were listening to a radio.

"**¿Qué pasa?**" Sofia asked.

"There was a big storm last night," Elena said.

"The electricity is out," Luisa

added.

"When will it come back?"

Sofia asked.

"We don't know," Papá said.

"The outage is widespread,"

the woman on the radio said.

"Be prepared for a night without

power."

"Oh, no!" Mamá said, worried.

"The refrigerator will get warm.

All the food will go bad."

"The yummy ice cream will melt,"
Luisa said.

"No, it won't." Sofia opened the
freezer. "We can eat it for breakfast."

Elena giggled. "Mamá and Papá will never let us do that."

"¿Por qué no?" Sofia said. "Is it better to throw it out?"

"Sofia has a point." Papá got spoons and bowls.

"Chocolate chip. My favorite!" Sofia said.

After the ice cream breakfast, everyone looked for flashlights. They only found one.

"Is this the only one we have?" Sofia asked.

"Sí," Mamá said.

Papá picked up his jacket. "I better go to the store."

"Can I come?" Sofia asked. "¿Por favor?"

"¡Vámonos!" Papá said, smiling.

CHAPTER 2

A Bright Idea

When they got to the store, the man at the counter said, "We are out of ice and flashlights."

"It's going to be a dark night for us," Papá said.

But Sofia saw something else they could use.

"Can we buy that pumpkin candle?" she asked.

"Why would we need a

Halloween candle?" Papá asked.

"It will help us see tonight,"

Sofia said.

"You are one smart girl, Sofia!"

Papá said.

Sofia looked at all the Halloween
items. Lots of them glowed in the dark.

"Papá," she said as she looked at
a big display. "Could we get some of
those? I have an idea."

She whispered her idea to **Papá**.
He smiled.

"**Muy bien**. The family will have
fun," he said.

On the way home, **Papá** stopped
by **Abuela's**.

"No light and no TV," **Abuela** said.

"Come home with us," Sofia said. "We are having a cookout."

"Family should be together when the power is out," Papá said.

"Gracias," Abuela said. "It is no fun to be in the dark."

"It could be," Sofia grinned.

Papá grinned, too.

"What are you two planning?"
Abuela asked.

"Just wait and see," Sofia said.

Back at home, Sofia walked across the yard to talk to her cousin, Hector.

"Can you bring your new drums over tonight?" she asked.

"Sí," Hector said. "Anything else you need?"

They searched the toy box. They found Manuel's fire truck and baby Mariela's duck on wheels.

"Alonzo has something good, too," Hector said. "I'll bring it."

Sofia rubbed her hands together. "Perfecto."

CHAPTER 3

Dancing in the Dark

That night, Hector's family came to Sofia's house.

"An October cookout!" Tío Miguel said. "Almost like summer!"

"Not even close," Hector said as he shivered. "In summer, I don't need a jacket."

"Go inside," Tía Carmen said.

"We will eat soon."

There were twelve people around the table, including baby Mariela in her high chair.

Mamá lit the pumpkin candle, but the food was still hard to see.

After dinner, Sofia invited

everyone into the living room.

Papá held up a sheet like a

curtain. Sofia disappeared behind it

and counted to three.

¡Uno...dos...tres!

"Ta-da!" Sofia yelled as she jumped out.

She was wearing glowing rings, bracelets, and earrings. She danced while Hector banged his toy drums. The drums had battery lights.

Mamá lit a candle on the piano.

Then she sat down and played a

salsa. Elena and Luisa clapped.

"Time to dance!" they yelled.

Tía Carmen grabbed Tío Miguel's hand. They started dancing. Tío Miguel was not a very good dancer, so it was extra funny.

Papá gave out glow-in-the-dark necklaces. Baby Mariela dragged her duck with the light-up wheels. Manuel switched on his fire truck. Alonzo waved his light saber.

Abuela sang and danced, too. She waved her glow-in-the-dark necklace in the air.

Then suddenly, the lights flickered. Everyone stopped. Then the lights flickered again. Suddenly, the room was filled with light.

"Hooray! The lights are back on!" Hector shouted.

"Turn them off!" Sofia cried.

"I'm already on my way to the light switch," Abuela said, smiling.

And just like that, the room was dark again.

"Time to party!" Sofia shouted as her whole family cheered.

Spanish Glossary

abuela — grandmother

gracias — thank you

mamá — mom

muy bien — very good

papá — dad

perfecto — perfect

por favor — please

por qué no — why not

qué pasa — what's wrong

sí — yes

tía — aunt

tío — uncle

uno, dos, tres — one, two, three

vámonos — let's go

Talk It Out

1. Sofia and her familiy ate ice cream for breakfast so it wouldn't melt. Do you think that was a good idea? Why or why not?

2. Did you know what Sofia was planning when she was at the store? Were there any clues in the story?

3. Do you think the author could have used a different holiday for the story?

Write It Down

1. What happens when the lights go out in your house? Talk to your parents about a plan, and write it down.

2. Make a list of five items you would include in an emergency kit for your family. If you have time, make one.

3. How do you think Sofia felt when she woke up and found out there was no electricity? Write a few sentences describing your answer.

About the Author

Jacqueline Jules is the award-winning author of thirty children's books, including *No English* (2012 Forward National Literature Award), *Zapato Power: Freddie Ramos Takes Off* (2010 Cybils Literary Award, Maryland Blue Crab Young Reader Honor Award, and ALSC Great Early Elementary Reads), and *Freddie Ramos Makes a Splash* (named on 2013 List of Best Children's Books of the Year by the Bank Street College Committee).

When not reading, writing, or teaching, Jacqueline enjoys time with her family in northern Virginia.

About the Illustrator

Kim Smith has worked in magazines, advertising, animation, and children's gaming. She studied illustration at the Alberta College of Art and Design in Calgary, Alberta.

Kim has illustrated several picture books, including *Home Alone: the Classic Illustrated Storybook* (Quirk Books), *Over the River and Through the Woods* (Sterling), and *A Ticket Around the World* (Owlkids Books). She lives in Calgary with her husband, Eric, and dog, Whisky.